The Adventures of
Eric Seagull
'Story-teller'

Caz Greenham

To Isabelle

Wishing You a Wonderful Christmas

Caz Greenham

SilverWood

Published in 2013 by the author using
SilverWood Books Empowered Publishing ®

SilverWood Books
30 Queen Charlotte Street, Bristol, BS1 4HJ
www.silverwoodbooks.co.uk

ISBN 978-1-78132-093-8 (paperback)
ISBN 978-1-78132-105-8 (ebook)

British Library Cataloguing in Publication Data
A CIP catalogue record for this book is available from the British Library

Set in Bembo by SilverWood Books
Printed on responsibly sourced paper

Dedication

In loving memory of my dearest dad, Johnny – Missing you Dad.

Love to mum Joan, my wonderful husband Geoff, and son-in-law Justin. Love to my beautiful daughters Claire and Emma. Grandchildren Kieran, Sophie, and Ethan.

1

Early Bird

Eric and his housemate Herbie were sleeping soundly in their beds beneath the quilted bed covers when Norman Mail Pigeon arrived. He hammered like a woodpecker with Eric's pebble doorknocker.

KNOCK! KNOCK! KNOCK! "Air-mail letter addressed to Eric Seagull, Rock-Face Nest, St. Mary's Bay, Brixham, in sunny South Devon," cooed Norman, wiping his hot brow on his purple braces.

No answer.

BANG! BANG! BANG! "Open the door!" Norman shrilled impatiently.

No reply.

"WAKEY! WAKEY! Lazy bones," Norman cooed. "It's time to get up. I know you can hear me," Norman coo-cooed again, his voice hoarse. His spindly legs were slowly bowing beneath the weight of his heavy green mailbag.

C-R-E-A-K! Using one toe, Eric lifted the rusty latch. As the door inched open, his beak appeared followed by a mop of untidy spiky

yellow hair. His bushy grey eyebrows arched. His eyes, black as a whale's fin, peered out as the early morning sun rose above the horizon. He blinked, stared, and blinked again as sea spray pounded like heavy rain against giant rocks below. He spotted fishing trawlers and sailing yachts rolling over foamy white waves heading towards Brixham Harbour.

Eric took hold of the blue envelope in his wing and thanked Norman for his mail. He then kicked his wonky, twiggy door shut.

As he glanced downwards at his Mickey-Mouse watch tied round his waist with orange fishing twine, he thought, *Norman's arrived early. I wonder why?*

Norman pressed his ear against Eric's door. "Joyful tidings, I hope?" he twittered, enquiringly.

No answer.

Crouching down on the ledge outside Eric's home, Norman waited for the next free current of warm air to come along. He leapt into it and caught a free sky-ride to his next coastal delivery. He swiftly disappeared behind a few bobtail clouds.

Eric and Herbie's nest is deep inside the hollow of giant rocks. It reaches high into the sky away from the outside world. Each summer Eric lays soft green meadow moss carpeting in all twelve rooms, and each spring paints the walls sunshine yellow.

Herbie is a tiny white mouse with enormous pink ears, and a nose that twitches all the time. He has twinkly pink eyes and a sunny smile. Herbie met Eric at the Ugliest Toad and Best Boogey Monster Competition, held at the fairy cave at Fishcombe Cove. He fell asleep in Eric's waistcoat pocket and has been the seagull's best friend, ever since.

Herbie's life couldn't be happier. He spent most days in the kitchen baking. His fruit-filled pancakes, ant fritters, deep-fried worms, and triple raspberry jam sandwiches are just a few of Eric's favourites.

Eric shrugged his wings. Glancing now and then at the mysterious envelope propped, unopened, against his bedside clock, he said to Herbie, "I wonder who it's from? Is it an early Christmas card? It's not my birthday until spring and it isn't Valentine's Day, either!"

"Tickle me whiskers," squeaked Herbie. "Open the envelope. Open it!"

Eric took hold of the envelope in his wings. He stared at it for a while, trying to guess what was inside. Then he placed it, unopened, beside his clock again. "Maybe Cousin Percy has invited me to go on his annual world tour. I've told you about Percy, haven't I, Herbie?" asked Eric.

"Yes, Eric, many times," replied Herbie, with a sigh. "Cousin Percy lives far away across the sea in Calais, France."

Tired and bored of listening to Eric's stories about his Cousin Percy, Herbie began washing his face and long whiskers with his paws. When the tinny kettle whistled on the iron stove in the kitchen, he made a pot of clover tea for them both. As they sipped their tea Herbie wanted to talk about Eric's envelope, but didn't. Then he went off and hung some curtains, and didn't ask. But finally, he couldn't hold it in any longer. He pretended not to care, but he was desperate to know, and asked, "I wonder what exciting news is inside your envelope, Eric? And why haven't you opened it, yet?"

Eric looked at his friend and said, "You should know by now, Herbie that I always try and guess what's inside my envelope before I open it."

Eric took hold of his envelope and ripped it open. A piece of waxy, shiny paper with fancy gold letters fluttered like a leaf to the floor. '

Herbie rushed to pick it up with his scrabbly paws. Eric took it from him, fixed his silver-wire reading specs onto his beak, narrowed his eyes, and read the scrawled message:

Cousin Percy is in trouble and needs your help
Go to him quickly
Signed...V

"Who is it from?" asked Herbie. "Who is it from?" he repeated excitedly.

Eric frowned. "I don't know...the corner of the page is missing. It's signed with the letter 'V'..."

2

Who Wrote the Letter?

"How mysterious," squeaked Herbie. His long whiskers twitched wildly. "What strange looking paper!"

Eric nodded and buttoned his stripy waistcoat. "I can't think of anyone whose name begins with 'V'. Can you, Herbie?"

Herbie thought hard. At last, he said, "No one at all."

Eric's head buzzed. "If Finny, the red haired leprechaun, wrote the letter, surely he would have signed off with an 'F'."

"What's a leper-thing-a-me, Eric?" asked Herbie, with a puzzled stare.

AHEM! Eric cleared his throat. "LEP-REEEE-CORNS, Herbie, look like woodland elves. They stand not much taller than a meadow flower and have pointy ears, and messy red hair. They wear brown breeches down to their knees and their long green coats have great big collars, and huge pockets..."

Yawning now and then, Herbie thought, *Oh no...another of Eric's boring explanations.* He then sat back on his haunches, trying his best not to doze off.

Eric thought a bit more and said, "Finny works all night as a shoemaker. He makes boots of red leather for the elves and slippers of fine cobwebs and moonbeams for the fairies. He is so rich that he stashes his gold in pots hidden at the end of a rainbow. He sleeps all day...or so they say."

Eric thought harder than ever about who might have sent his envelope. He read his letter with its fancy gold writing over and over, again.

"What are you going to do, Eric?" asked Herbie.

"I must visit the Fairy King and Queen at Fishcombe Cove. They have special magic that could help Cousin Percy," explained Eric.

Herbie smiled, and said, "I would come along for the ride, but you know me...I get sick after just one of your sky-dives, Eric."

Eric stared at Herbie and said, "No mouse house parties with those street mice while I'm gone, mind. Instead, when I return from my adventure to save Cousin Percy, we will celebrate by having the best-ever Fancy Dress Party. We'll invite all our friends and relatives."

Herbie's eyes twinkled playfully. His head filled with thoughts of partying with his many mouse friends. And so, he crept off to the front room to write his party list. He took a box of matches from the mantle above the fireplace, struck a long matchstick with its blue tip, and carefully lit the log fire.

As the fire snapped, crackled and popped, curls of wood smoke chuffed and puffed from the crooked chimney pot. Herbie curled up in his mouse armchair. His eyelids got heavy, and he drifted into a deep mouse-nap. Snoring beside the cosy fire, he dreamed his best-ever party dream.

3

Eric's Lucky Blue Trilby Hat

CRASH! BASH! THUMP!

"What's all that noise?" asked Herbie, his whiskers trembling. He shot a sideways glance at Eric's watch and said, "I've only had forty winks. A mouse needs his beauty sleep, you know."

"Not at two o'clock in the afternoon when I've lost my hat," replied Eric. "I've emptied cupboard after cupboard and four biscuit tins. I can't find my lucky blue trilby hat anywhere," he huffed. "Now, where did I put it?"

"Is this what you are looking for?" asked Herbie, tugging on the rim of a hat wedged behind his armchair.

"Thanks," Eric huffed again, taking it from him.

Finally, his hat, with its deep sunken crown, a pinch at the front, and narrow brim, balanced on his head. Pulling funny faces at his reflection in a shiny sardine tin hanging from a nail on the bathroom wall, Eric nudged his hat, sideways. "Mmm, mmm! Nice fit," he beamed. Taking his hat off again, he plucked a few loose feathers from his wing and stuck them to the brim.

"This really is my lucky hat, Herbie," said Eric, smiling into the mirror one last time. "I wore it the night I met Fairy Bluebelle at the Fairy Ball. And Mr Cormorant Seabird offered me the job as Storyteller for The Brixham Times newspaper that same night."

To make certain his hat didn't blow off his head during his flight to

Fishcombe Cove, Eric tied it on with fishing twine, making a bow beneath his chin.

Wiping away cobwebs that clung to his red flying goggles, he pulled them on over his spiky hair. All ready to go, with his envelope tucked safely inside his yellow satchel, his tummy tightened like a sailor's knot at the thought of the perilous journey ahead. He took a deep breath, and hopped to the edge of his nest...

...and jumped onto a passing free warm air current. Swiftly, he rose higher and higher into the sky. His best friend, Herbie, waving at him from far below, swiftly grew smaller and smaller.

Eric waved back, squawking excitedly, "I'm on my way to Fishcombe Cove!" before disappearing behind a fish-shaped cloud.

Eric hadn't flown far before he felt something wasn't quite right. Instead of going forward, he seemed to be going backward, and sideways, then up and down. From nowhere, a furious gale sprung up and the sky looked full of inky black clouds. Eric flapped fiercely, but made little progress.

All of a sudden, with a mighty BOOM! And a flash of light, the world exploded around him. Rain pelted his wings and the sky flashed and thundered. Deafened, Eric found his wings seizing up. He plummeted from the sky down to the raging waves of the English Channel, far below.

4

Eric and the Sea Monster

Hurtling towards the ocean, Eric crossed his six toes for good luck.

"HELP! HELP! HELP!" he squawked. "I promise I'll never tie Herbie's whiskers in a knot again. And I won't say no to mouse house parties, either. Please don't let me drown," he wept, as he got closer and closer to the sea below.

BUMP! SQUISH! SKID!

Landing shakily, Eric found himself sitting astride the back of a huge, wet, and slippery sea monster. "Aah," he gasped. "I'm saved!"

SWHISS-SSS-SSSH! SWHOOO-OOO-OOOSH! "If you want a ride simply ask," said a deep voice. "I'm Harry Whale. Tell me who you are?" he asked his passenger.

The enormous whale suddenly shot seawater out of his double blowholes. Two big fountains whizzed upwards high into the sky,

before splattering back down into the sea soaking Eric. *I wish I had an umbrella*, he thought.

Eric's feathers looked a mess stuck together with sticky, salty seawater. "It's only me…Eric Seagull. I'm Storyteller for The Brixham Times newspaper. Nice to meet you, Harry," he said, hoping the sea monster wasn't going to dive beneath the waves.

Harry looked upwards. Glancing over his shoulder at Eric's sea-sprayed goggles, he asked, "What brings you so far out to sea on such a windy day, Eric?"

"Well, Harry…" began Eric slipping and sliding on the whale's wet back. He tried telling him about his blue envelope and his best friend Herbie, who always got sick whenever he went for a sky-ride.

The whale stayed silent and listened to Eric with interest.

"So you see, Harry, Cousin Percy needs my help."

Eric told Harry that he heard a rumour the day before at The Breakwater Beach. He heard that the Fairy King and Queen have special powers. "I'm hopeful the fairies' magic will help Cousin Percy."

"What powers, Eric?" asked the baffled whale, who knew nothing about fairy magic.

Eric grabbed hold of a twig bobbing about amongst the foamy white waves. Wrapping his claws around it, he waved his twiggy wand in the air. "This is what fairies do," he told Harry. "They say funny words like 'wazzywoo, wippywee-ee, and whoozz-oo.' My friend, Fairy Bluebelle, shows me magic tricks all the time when I visit her at the fairy cave," he explained. "Trouble is, Belle's magic isn't all that powerful."

Harry shot two more big spouts of water out of his blowholes. Blinking his small piercing black eyes, he told Eric, "I have a friend who is a Mermaid Queen. She lives in a palace beneath the waves and sees most things that happen in the world. She's magical, too."

Before Harry could finish his tale, Eric lost his balance and slipped from the creature's wet back, for Harry didn't have ears he could grip.

SPLASH! Eric plunged into the cold-as-ice ocean, deeper than the highest mountain.

5

The Mer-Creatures

GLUG! GLUG! GLUG!

A dazed Eric sank like a stone to the ocean bed. He stared through his goggles at the strange world beneath the waves. Eric was born with three toes on each foot, instead of webbed feet like his seagull friends. He couldn't swim a single stroke, which meant one thing: deep trouble!

Eric's throat filled with seawater. Choking, he thrashed his legs and wings praying to find the sea's surface again. *I wish I had learnt to swim,* he thought.

Suddenly, a stream of bubbles appeared from nowhere. They wrapped themselves round him from his wet mop of hair to his six toes. As the bubbles burst and disappeared, he found he could breathe again.

Eric stood on the ocean floor, lifted one foot and scratched his beak. Something he always did when he felt puzzled. *Those were magic bubbles*, he thought.

Blinking, staring, and blinking again, he spotted a towering building made of glass in the distance. *This looks like the palace Harry Whale told me about before I slipped from his back*, he thought.

A puzzled Eric walked towards the large building. It was a long way, but on and on he trudged. At last, he stood outside the palace's tall golden gates with its massive pillars. Peering through a large window, he noticed a merman and mermaid sitting on shell-shaped thrones. They were wearing silver crowns glistening with sparkly jewels. *Reminds me of the stars in the night sky above my rock-face nest*, he thought.

Unaware that Eric Seagull's prying eyes watched their every swish-of-a-tail, the Sea King and Queen nattered away as mer-creatures do.

Eric gasped with fear as a sailfish with its large sail-shaped fin swam past his goggles. A shark plodded by on its fins. Fish stared curiously at his blue hat, while brown sea snails slithered up his long yellow beak.

Before Eric could say, 'mouth-watering cod fish', he found himself trapped like a tinned sardine and unable to move. Hundreds of sea creatures crowded him. Cucumber-shaped fish pushed and shoved

trying to get a glimpse of the feathery visitor.

"Don't tickle!" Eric pleaded. "I hate being tickled."

WHOOP! WHOOP! WHOOP! Echoed through the undercurrent. Eric caught a glimpse of mer-creatures through the palace window. He watched them blow into shell-shaped horns. They were summoning their servant fish back into the palace.

Free at last, he noticed a kitchen in a far corner. *Looks a bit like Herbie's kitchen*, he thought.

Large brown crabs with happy faces trimmed green seaweed salad with their sharp pincer claws. Flying fish spooned slimy black fish eggs into empty oyster shells.

Must be tea-time, Eric thought, licking his lips.

An octopus with rows of suckers and an oval body wore a chef's hat on his enormous head. Eric watched in wonderment as he chopped, sliced, and diced sea cucumbers and large purple mushrooms with his eight arms.

A hermit crab carrying a whelk shell suddenly scampered across Eric's toes. "Ah! Don't tickle!" He laughed for the first time since arriving in this strange world beneath the waves.

From nowhere, a huge dark shape zigzagged its way through the shadowy waters heading straight for the unsuspecting Eric.

6

A Mermaid's Dinner?

"Found you at last, Eric," said Harry Whale. "I've been searching the ocean for you. That friend of mine…the one I was telling you about before you slipped from my back…is Mermaid Queen Violet. She's queen of all the seas. This is her underwater kingdom. I have been friends with the Sea Queen and her relatives for as long as I can remember," he explained. He then stared curiously at bubbles bursting out from Eric's nostrils.

Harry burst out laughing. "If I didn't know better, Eric, I would say you were turning into a mer-gull."

Eric pulled a funny face at his friend, but didn't answer.

As the water swirled, Mermaid Queen Violet appeared. Eric gazed in amazement at the most dazzling magical being. Her pretty face made him think of Fairy Bluebelle, while her gleaming turquoise scaly tail was like that of an exotic fish. Her skin looked whiter than foam on the edge of the waves at St. Mary's Bay. Her ocean blue eyes deep as the sea, and her long golden hair flowed loosely down her back.

The mermaid fixed her gaze on Eric. She swam towards him until they were nose-to-beak.

Eric's legs trembled with fear. "Seagulls aren't a bit tasty!" he said with a shiver. "I haven't got much meat on my ole bones. Please nice mermaid, don't eat me!" he pleaded.

17

Harry watched his friend tremble with fear. "Mermaids don't eat seagulls, Eric. Or, so they say," he said with a smile and a wink.

Swishing her powerful tail, the Mermaid Queen quivered with laughter. "I saw your beak pressed up against my palace window earlier. I am Queen Violet and I rule the world beneath the waves. And no… mermaids don't eat seagulls," she said with a friendly smile.

Eric listened wide-eyed to the lively sea creature.

"In my magical underwater kingdom I see most things that happen in the world through my looking glass," Queen Violet explained. "It was I who wrote to you on my special sea paper."

So the 'V' at the bottom of my letter stood for Violet, Eric thought. *Wait 'til Herbie finds out that my letter came from a Sea Queen!*

Queen Violet went on. "I met Cousin Percy two fishing seasons ago. I found him stranded on giant rocks close to Berry Head Lighthouse. He was entangled in fishing twine left behind by careless holidaymakers. He looked so sorry for himself that I set him free. And more recently, my servants heard a rumour that Cousin Percy needed help of a different kind. That's why I wrote to you. After sealing my letter inside its blue envelope I tucked it safely inside Norman Mail Pigeon's mailbag while he rested on rocks at Brixham Harbour," she explained.

Eric's bushy grey eyebrows arched. "Could you please tell me, Your Mer-Majester, why Cousin Percy needs help, again?" he asked curiously.

Queen Violet shook her head and said, "I'm not quite sure. The flying fish who brought me the message forgot most of it by the time they arrived. And my looking glass can be a bit fickle at times…it can't always be relied upon. You should go and ask the Fairy King and Queen at Fishcombe Cove. They can find out most things with their special magic."

Swishing her scaly tail Queen Violet told Eric, "King Edmund is busy teaching Rico the octopus how to string saltwater pearls onto golden thread. I'm certain that a pearl necklace would make a perfect present for the Fairy Queen."

Wearing several necklaces herself, the friendly mermaid placed two strands of the cloud looking gems round Eric's neck and said, "A gift for the Fairy Queen."

Eric's eyes widened in amazement. "Thank you, Your Mer-Majester," he replied.

Queen Violet handed Eric a golden comb. "A gift for the Fairy King's wild, curly hair," she said with a smile.

Eric thanked her again.

As Eric gazed in wonderment at little fish flipping soft sand with their fins, he began to daydream of life beneath the waves. *If I could be a fish in the ocean I would be bigger than Harry Whale, and have amazing fins*, he thought.

"Careful what you wish for, Eric," giggled Queen Violet, making it her business to know her visitor's thoughts. "I have a *Book of Spells* in the library. I am certain I can find a spell that can change you into the most handsome fish. I haven't used spells for over a hundred years, but I'll give it my best shot," she said willingly.

"Oh, no…" began Eric, "I…"

Although Queen Violet had good intentions, she couldn't resist performing magic. She did her utmost to tempt the seagull. "Don't waste time day-dreaming, Eric. I just know you would make a fine-looking fish…perhaps a handsome swordfish," she smiled. "Plenty of time to save Cousin Percy later."

Eric laughed and said, "Reminds me of the time I watched a show at The Palace Theatre. Two big, black as night, hairy rats with warty faces, knobby feet, and dressed in shabby brown cloaks sword fenced on stage. The champion fencer was called Eric the Great!" he beamed.

Eric thought hard. At last, he shook his head, and said, "No! Cousin Percy is in deep trouble and needs my help. I must continue my journey to the Fairy King and Queen's cave at Fishcombe Cove. Then, after I have saved Cousin Percy, I will fly home to my rock-face nest and write about my adventures for my newspaper. For if I don't I could lose my job as Storyteller for The Brixham Times," he said with a stare. *I would hate that to happen to me*, he thought.

Eric followed Queen Violet's servants into the library. *I wonder what type of book a Mermaid Queen would read*, he thought gazing at hundreds of books stacked on the many shelves.

As the fish searched for *The Book of Spells*, Eric noticed an age-old book poking out from behind a giant clamshell. *Bet this is what they are looking for!* he thought tugging on the well-worn purple cover with black curly writing. Curiously, Eric flicked through the pages with his wing until he reached *Untried Short Spells ~ Beware*.

Queen Violet appeared and took the book from him. Without much thought, she began reading from the page "IZZZ-Y! WAZZZ-Y! OOZZZ-Y! WIZZZZZ-Y! SW-OORD-FISS-SHY!"

"STOP," shouted Eric worriedly.

Too late!

A curious blue light circled Eric. Magical silver and gold droplets of rain showered down upon his head, which made him shiver. *I feel as cold as a codfish!* he thought.

7

Eric the Swordfish

Eric's beak twitched and shrunk before disappearing. In its place grew a long swordfish jaw. His feathers fell out and floated away in the sea's undercurrent. Fins replaced his wings. He glanced downwards and wiggled his toes, for they were still on the end of his skinny ankles.

"Oopsy!" whispered Queen Violet with a frown.

Staring at his reflection in the palace window, Eric hollered, "I'm not a seagull! I'm not a fish! I'm nothing!"

"Look on the bright side," said Queen Violet. "You have great fins, a handsome sword-like jaw, and now you can swim. Something you couldn't do when you were a seagull."

Eric's odd look brought him many admirers, for on his back and all the way down his spine grew a handsome fin. His razor sharp long jaw could slice through the thickest driftwood.

Eric was just getting used to his strange appearance when two pretty dolphins began giggling from behind a nearby rock.

Dread welled up inside Eric's tummy. He said to Queen Violet, "I hate being a freaky fish."

Queen Violet tried her best to change Eric back into his seagull form, but none of her spells worked.

Harry Whale had been listening to the goings-on from the shadows of an old shipwreck, and said, "I have a great idea, Eric. Why don't you join the travelling Ocean Circus? It's due to arrive tomorrow afternoon. Master Dolphin is the owner and he told me just last week that he is always on the lookout for new talent like yours. You could be a megastar, a superstar. A trillion starfish could light up your name. You could be a shining star attraction."

Eric was speechless. He stared back at Harry in amazement and thought, *I don't want to be famous. I'm on an adventure to save Cousin Percy. And now it's all gone horribly wrong!*

Crabs, fish, and anemones gathered round and chattered all at once urging Eric to join the Circus. His head filled with the sea creatures babbling, squeaky voices making him almost topple over. He could see the crowds and hundreds of fans applauding his strange appearance. *A circus life is not for me*, he thought.

Queen Violet appeared carrying *The Book of Spells* under her arm. "I'll try and find a spell that will change you back into a seagull, Eric," she told him. "Unless you want to live as a fish in my underwater kingdom?" she asked cheekily.

"NOT LIKELY!" snapped Eric.

Queen Violet flicked through the pages of her *Book of Spells* until she found *Fix a Spell*. "Um…this looks hopeful," she said. "I'll give this spell a try." She began reading aloud from the page, "SW-II-SSSS-SSH-Y! SW-OOOO-SS-SS-HHY! SS-EEA-GULL-LL-Y! FIXXXX-MEEEEE!"

All at once, Queen Violet's spell worked. Before Eric could say, 'mouthwatering shell fish,' he had changed back into his seagull form. He looked as good as ever.

"Thanks," said Eric checking his feathers were all there.

"I'll swim with you back to the sea's surface, Eric," said Harry.

"That would be great," Eric agreed.

Eric waved goodbye to Queen Violet, and scrambled onto Harry's huge back. Together they swam to the sea's surface.

No longer used to breathing fresh air, Eric struggled to get his breath. "Phewee," he gasped as jets of seawater spurted from his beak.

Sitting across Harry's double blowholes, Eric straightened his blue trilby hat. He pulled away slimy sea snails stuck to his flying goggles, and emptied seawater from his yellow satchel.

SLIP! SLURP! SLIDE! WHACK! "If only you weren't so slippery, Harry!" huffed Eric, unable to clamber to his feet.

"Oh, Harry! I'll never be able to take off, and if that happens I'll never get to Fishcombe Cove, or save Cousin Percy," he said flumping down with a sigh.

8

Airborne at Last

SWH-OO-OOSH! SWHI-SSH! SWH-OO-OOSH!

Harry looked upwards and without thinking, he shot jets of seawater through his double blowholes.

Eric found himself propelled upwards high into the sky. He balanced on the top of the waterspout flapping his wings like crazy.

"WH-OO-PP-EE," he screeched as he rose higher and higher. "Clear the skies. I'm taking off." Looking downwards, he called out, "Harry…you're the cleverest whale in the ocean."

Harry smiled and blinked back.

Airborne at last, Eric frantically flapped his powerful wings, but he didn't get far in the stormy sky. Gloomy grey clouds spun all around him.

Circling in the sea below, Harry concerned for his friend watched helplessly. "I'll catch you if you fall from the sky," he shouted out, hoping Eric could hear.

Eric, almost giving up any hope of continuing with his journey, suddenly shot forward, for a gust of wind took hold of his wings sending him on his way.

"HOORAY!" Eric clucked. "I'M ON MY WAY TO FISHCOMBE COVE." As he glanced downwards, he squawked, "Goodbye Harry Whale. Thanks for being such a good friend."

Harry spurted one final farewell jet of water high into the air, before diving beneath the waves.

Later that afternoon, cool winds blew the dark clouds away. Eric found himself soaring towards the scorching sun. His soggy inner feathers began drying too quickly. "Ouch! I'm burning up," he screeched.

Spinning out of control, his heart pounded like a drum inside his chest. *Let me think! Let me think! I'll cross my toes for good luck*, he thought.

Before Eric could say, 'lip-smacking mackerel,' the plucky seagull landed safely on the beach at Fishcombe Cove. He stared downwards as his feet sank beneath the soft white sand. Sweat rolled down his beak. His feathery cheeks turned red with exertion. He fished a hanky from his waistcoat pocket and mopped his sweaty brow. *Perfect landing*, he thought. *What an adventurous day this is turning into and it isn't over yet.*

9

Fishcombe Cove

SWISH! ZOOM! Eric flew like a feathery jet plane through an entrance into the fairy cave only known to seagulls. He arrived outside the heavy wooden door of the royal Throne Room and pulled his trilby hat straight. He then tugged away straggly seaweed still hooked to the side of his flying goggles. Using one toe, he pressed the golden doorbell. Before its tinkly musical notes faded away, the King and Queen of all the fairies appeared. They stood not much taller than a wild flower.

Eric lifted his hat, peeled off his goggles and bowed before the royal fairies. He rubbed his eyes, for his goggles always left red weals on his face. He presented the Fairy Queen with the pearl necklace, and handed the King a golden comb for his wild, curly hair. "Gifts from Mermaid Queen Violet," he explained. "Queen of all the seas."

"Please thank Her Majesty when you next visit her underwater realm," said the King and Queen, unaware that Eric nearly drowned, or got turned into a freaky swordfish-gull getting the gifts in the first place.

Eric followed the royal couple inside the candlelit room. The Fairy Queen's long gown swished, while the King's suit of golden thread sparkled as they flew onto their golden thrones.

Eric flopped down on a purple stool beside the marble fireplace. He glanced upwards, for above his head, hanging from the cave ceiling, he noticed the most magnificent tree-shaped crystal hanging light. Its many branches were bejeweled with teardrop lights that sparkled in sunlight peeping through a closed window.

Wow! This is a magical place! Eric thought.

The Fairy Queen rang her tinkly bell. "Tea-time," she announced.

Four tiny elves with silky gossamer wings flew in. They each carried a silver tray heaped with jammy biscuits, cakes, and sugared almonds; the King's favourite tea-time treats.

Mmm, mmm raspberry jam. These taste like Herbie's triple jam sandwiches, Eric thought licking crumbs from his beak with his long tongue.

"Tell me, Eric, what brings you to our cave today?" asked the King munching a biscuit.

"It would please me greatly, Your Majesters, if you would read my letter," Eric replied. "My Cousin Percy lives in France and he's in deep trouble." He then reached inside his yellow satchel, pulled out his blue envelope, and handed it to the Queen.

Both fairies read the letter and sweetly smiled. After a bit of careful thinking they gave their opinion. "We fear our magic isn't powerful enough. It may not reach across the sea to France," they agreed.

Eric raised his bushy grey eyebrows. "But, Your Majesters, I heard a rumour that the Fairy Truths and Spells Fountain holds the most powerful magic in all the land."

"And so it does," giggled the King. "What a dazzling idea!" He wiggled his pointy ears, twirled his curls round his finger, and said,

"Why didn't we think of that my Queen? We can be such scatter-brain fairies, at times!"

The Queen sweetly smiled at the King and waved her silver wand in the air.

Eric stared in wonderment as a flurry of sparkly dust swirled in the air. It lifted them off the ground and transported them to the royal garden with its magical fountain.

Eric's eyes blinked, stared, and blinked again as he stood beside the King and Queen in their sun-filled garden. The Queen clapped her hands twice. The fountain's jet of rainbow water shot high into the air before spreading outward in a wide circle, which filled the pool to the brim.

As they waited for the waters to settle, Eric peered in. "This reminds me of a film I once watched at The Brixham Cinema," he said.

In the waters, Herbie was partying with his street mice friends. They were singing and dancing to music in their Ballroom at St Mary's Bay ~ only used on special occasions.

As the images of his friend faded away, the waters showed Cousin Percy and Finny quarrelling. They stood atop the tall Calais Lighthouse in France with its dazzling light shining out to sea.

"Push my shoulder like that once more, Finny, and I'll peck that stubby nose off your freckly face!" Cousin Percy warned folding his wings across his feathery chest.

PUSH! SHOVE! TUSSLE! SLAP!

"Freckles! Leprechauns don't have freckles! Feather face!" yelled Finny throwing a final punch at Cousin Percy.

10

The Stone Seagull

"Finders' keepers," teased Finny. "I found the pot of gold coins under a pile of pebbles on the beach so the gold belongs to me…you feather duster," he laughed.

"You red haired mop-head," laughed Cousin Percy. "That pile of pebbles, as you call it, happens to be my nest. The pebbles and the gold belong to me. That's final!" He gave a huge *harrumph*, which ruffled his feathers like a windy Force 10 gale. Folding his wings across his chest, he cheekily smiled at Finny.

Cousin Percy and Finny have been friends for a long time. While they bickered most days over treasure found on the beach, they always patched up their friendship long before bedtime. And so, today seemed like any other day. Or, was it?

Finny stood almost as tall as Cousin Percy did in his half-laced brown leather boots. He hopped from one foot to the other. His hands curled into fists as his face turned red with fury, which clashed with his hair.

"Keep the pebbles," Finny hollered in his piercing tone. "Just han' o'er that gold." His bony fingers uncurled as he reached into the pocket of his long green velvet coat with its big collar. He pulled out a golden pouch bursting with sparkly dust, and waved it in the air. "Tis your last chance Percy," he fumed.

Cousin Percy covered his ears with his wings and began to sing, "La, la, la, la, la, la, la, la, la, la," ignoring Finny.

"Last chance! Final chance!" raged Finny.

"Ah non! Not in a mill-ion, trill-ion years," squawked Cousin Percy.

Finny couldn't hold back his fiery anger any longer. He shook the magic dust over Cousin Percy. He then stood back, watched, and waited to see what would happen.

A burst of seagull shaped sparkly dust swirled in the air. Cousin Percy magically tingled from his fuzzy orange hair down to his toes, before turning into a stone statue.

From nowhere another seagull appeared. It landed on Cousin Percy's head and did what seagulls do naturally: it cheekily poo-pooed all over his smart navy beret!

11

The Fairy King and Queen's Rules

Delighted at his victory, Finny leapt in the air kicking his heels together. Playing a bouncy tune on his flute, he danced and jigged his way back to his shoemaker's shop in the town.

Standing beside the fairies' magic fountain, Eric stared at the picture in the water. He checked the seagull statue for any signs of life, and asked, "Is Cousin Percy dead?" As the image disappeared, he added, "Please kind fairies help save my Cousin."

The Fairy King stared at Eric. As he twisted his curls round his thumb, he said, "This is far more serious than we first thought."

Eric nodded in agreement.

Pacing up and down, Eric said, "The Truths and Spells Fountain showed us that the gold coins were found under pebbles on a beach. It's well-known that seagulls throughout the land own all the beaches. Surely that must mean Cousin Percy is the rightful owner of the gold?" He asked hopefully.

"How spiffily clever!" said the King.

The Fairy Queen nodded in agreement.

"We declare that the gold belongs to Cousin Percy," agreed the fairies.

"Thank you, Your Majesters," said Eric with a happy smile.

Reaching into a hidden pocket in her silky gown, the Fairy Queen pulled out an extra-special pouch of sparkly dust she kept for such emergencies. She handed the pouch to Eric with a smile that never left her face.

"It's just possible that my magic dust might put an end to Cousin Percy and Finny's squabbling...but...it has never been used on a stone statue of a seagull. Try it and see. You must shake half the dust over Cousin Percy," she explained. "Then, you must find the shoemaker's shop in the town and sprinkle the other half over Finny. Off you go. We will watch what happens in the Truths and Spells Fountain."

"Thank you, Your Majester," said Eric. "I will fly faster than any seagull in sunny South Devon." He then placed the pouch of magic dust inside his waistcoat pocket for safekeeping. He flapped his powerful wings and took off. He flew like a feathery jet plane until he reached the harbour in France. Circling high in the sky, his watchful eyes searched for Cousin Percy. He knew it wasn't going to be easy. He looped the loop and did several sky dives. He couldn't see him anywhere.

Suddenly, a murky sea mist drifted across the ocean. It rose higher and higher gripping Eric's throat tightly.

COUGH! COUGH! COUGH! Eric choked. Flapping his wings like crazy, he fell like a stone from the sky. His wing crashed to the ground. He pulled down hard and rose steadily upwards into the sky again. *Thank goodness I listened in class to wise owl Tutor Polly at The Seagull Academy*, he thought.

A fresh sea breeze blew the fog away. Eric glanced downwards and spotted Cousin Percy below wearing a concrete overcoat. With another seagull standing on his head, his eyes seemed to say, 'Hurry up, please!'

Eric zoomed downwards to where Cousin Percy stood encased in concrete. He shook some sparkly dust out of the packet onto his head. In an instant Cousin Percy's eyes blinked, his wings flapped and the seagull using him as a perch took off in a hurry!

"Thanks Eric. How did you…?" he began, flapping his wings like crazy.

"No time to waste… got to find Finny…catch up with you later when you've got rid of the cement dust from your wings," Eric screeched.

Finny proved much harder to find. Eric waddled up and down every cobbled street in the town until his feet ached. He peered through every shoemaker's shop window searching for Finny. He couldn't see him anywhere. His wings were heavy and scuffing the ground when, at last, he arrived outside the last shoemaker's shop window in the town, in the last cobbled street.

Eric peered in. Row upon row of fairy boots and shoes in all shapes, sizes, and colours crowded the shelves awaiting collection by their owners. Still there was no sign of Finny. He couldn't see anyone.

Eric pushed open the shop door, which made the brass bell hanging above it jingle merrily. No one appeared. He crept through the shop, pulled aside a checkered curtain that hung across an archway at the back, which led to a back room. At last, he found Finny curled up fast asleep in his wooden bed and snoring loudly. Eric carried out the Fairy King and Queen's orders. As he shook the remaining magic dust over the sleeping leprechaun, he whispered, "Finny…when you next see Cousin Percy, you'll apologise for stealing from him,

and turning him to stone…" He then tiptoed out of the shop smiling; delighted that he had carried out the fairies' royal commands.

Hunger pangs began to gurgle noisily inside Eric's tummy. *I'll fly to the harbour to catch a mackerel fish,* he thought. Suddenly, something took hold of his tail. Try as he may, he couldn't take off.

12

Will Percy get His Feathers Back?

SQUAWK! SQUAWK! SQUAWK! Eric protested. Spinning round, he came beak to beak with his feathery Cousin Percy.

Cousin Percy smoothed down his blue T-shirt. His navy beret perched flat on his head. "I've come to find Finny," he told Eric. "I haven't seen him all day."

"Don't you remember?" asked Eric. "You and Finny argued over a pot of gold, earlier."

"What gold? What fight?" asked a bewildered Cousin Percy. "I remember turning to stone, and then you, Eric, rescuing me."

Eric laughed. He could see that the powerful magic dust had removed Cousin Percy's memory over the gold and his quarrel with Finny, earlier.

Eric and Cousin Percy flapped their wide wings as they prepared to take off. Almost airborne a tinkly voice yelled after them in the distance.

"ERIC! PERCY!" Shouted Finny. "Wait! Wait for me! Don't go without me! Take me with you!"

The seagulls skidded to a halt. Cousin Percy glanced over his shoulder and spotted Finny, his short legs running as fast as they could run.

"Can I come along for a sky-ride?" he hollered, his cheeks rosy red.

Finny clambered onto Cousin Percy's back, and told him, "I'm so sorry Percy, it was wrong of me to steal from you. I didn't mean to turn you to stone."

Cousin Percy smiled back at Finny and winked, but didn't answer. Then, the three friends took off to the skies.

Flying behind puffy clouds, they looped the loop, did a figure of eight, and a figure of nine. Cousin Percy glanced sideways at Eric and asked him, "How long are you in town for? I am off on a world tour at dawn with the local seagulls. Do you want to come along? It'll be great fun."

"No thanks," Eric chuckled. "I've had enough adventure for one day...maybe next year."

Cousin Percy glanced over his shoulder at Finny, and asked, "Do you want to come along on my tour? It'll be great fun. Loads of sky-rides."

"You bet!" replied Finny, his cheeks glowing redder and redder.

After their sky-ride, the three friends feasted on a fish supper at the harbour.

Eric glanced downwards at his Mickey-Mouse watch, still tied round his waist with fishing twine, and said, "It's getting late. Time I flew home to my rock-face nest. I must write about my travels before bedtime for The Brixham Times newspaper. For if I don't, Mr Cormorant Seabird might sack me." *I don't want to lose my job*, he thought.

Finny munched the last shrimp. He

waved goodbye to his friends, and merrily hopped, skipped, and whistled a jingly tune on his flute. He made his way back to his shoemaker's shop in the town.

A tired Finny arrived home. He went inside his shop, shut the door, and hung his coat on a hook behind his bedroom door. His feet were hot and blistered. He was too tired to make a hot milky drink, so he climbed into his wooden bed with its feather-filled mattress and pillow. Sleepily, he snuggled down beneath the covers.

Snoring loudly, Finny forgot one thing: he went to bed wearing his half-laced brown leather boots. They stuck out from beneath his green quilt at the bottom of his bed.

After that, Cousin Percy and Finny always share treasure they find on the beach, and never squabble.

13

Home Sweet Home

Eric waved goodbye to Cousin Percy, before flying home to his rock-face nest at St. Mary's Bay, Brixham, in sunny South Devon. "I'm home," he screeched bursting in through the twiggy, wonky front door.

"Ooh! I was just tidying up," squeaked Herbie, sweeping crumbs under the sofa with his long tail. Something all mice do!

"Did you have any mouse parties while I've been away, Herbie?" asked Eric with a stare.

"Who me?" replied Herbie with a sunny smile.

As the best friends finished off triple raspberry jam sandwiches leftover from breakfast, Herbie curled up in his cosy mouse armchair to listen to Eric's fantastical adventures.

"Did you bring me a gift from your travels?" asked Herbie leaping inside Eric's waistcoat pocket. "Ooh, what's all this glittery stuff?" he asked, sniffing and snuffling with his pink nose.

Before Eric could give any kind of answer, Herbie's whiskers quivered and his body tingled from his furry head down to his scrabbly paws. Poking his head out of Eric's pocket, Herbie's nose was no longer plain pink, for it glowed fluorescent pink. Now, he would always be seen in the dark.

That same night, Eric wrote mind-blowing stories about his travels, by candlelight, while sitting at his desk in the library. They made front-page news for *The Brixham Times* newspaper the following day. Eric's Boss, Mr Cormorant Seabird, simply would not believe it all happened. But, his thousands of readers know that it *did* happen…right?

Eric has received another letter delivered by Norman Mail Pigeon. It's an invitation inviting him to talk about his underwater adventures on a television chat show.

Make sure you don't miss it!

THE END

About the Author

I'm Caz, short for Carole, born in South-Bristol and married to Geoff. I have two grown-up daughters and three grandchildren. I like all types of music, writing, reading, photography, gardening, yoga, and dog walking. My passion for adventure books began when I was just five years old, but I didn't begin writing my own childrens' books until I purchased my first laptop in 2009.

I admire greatly the works of Hans Christian Andersen, Charles Dickens and The Brothers Grimm. I worked as an audio-secretary in offices around the Bristol City Centre for many years. The idea for my books came to me during a holiday in Torbay walking our cocker spaniels. A cheeky herring gull with spiky hair glared at me as I walked past. I knew in an instant that a quirky seagull would be my main character in my books.

I began writing *The Adventures of Eric Seagull* that afternoon. My character is named after a flamboyant Professor of Physics who worked with my dearest dad during the 1970s. His messy yellow tufts, bushy grey eyebrows, colourful waistcoat and bow tie matched my seagull's description perfectly. (He asked me to dance once, but I turned him down!)

For more about Caz and Eric, you can visit Caz's website at:
www.cazgreenham.com

CPSIA information can be obtained at www.ICGtesting.com
Printed in the USA
LVOW021143110313

3415LVUK00002B/3/P

9 781781 320938